GUS and GRANDPA
at Basketball

Claudia Mills ★ Pictures by Catherine Stock

Farrar, Straus and Giroux

New York

For Asher Bensko,
who shared our first basketball season
—C.M.

For Joe
—C.S.

Text copyright © 2001 by Claudia Mills
Illustrations copyright © 2001 by Catherine Stock
Distributed in Canada by Douglas & McIntyre Ltd.
Color separations by Phoenix Color Corporation
Printed and bound in the United States of America by Phoenix Color Corporation
First edition, 2001
1 3 5 7 9 10 8 6 4 2

Library of Congress Cataloging-in-Publication Data
Mills, Claudia.
    Gus and Grandpa at basketball / Claudia Mills ; pictures by
Catherine Stock.— 1st ed.
        p.   cm.
    Summary: Gus enjoys basketball practice, but the noise and
pace of real games bother him, until his grandpa gives him some
good advice.
    ISBN 0-374-32818-8
    [1. Basketball—Fiction. 2. Grandfathers—Fiction.] I. Stock,
Catherine, ill. II. Title.

PZ7.M63963 Gudi 2001
[E]—dc21   00-37646

Contents

Basketball Practice

Swish!
The basketball fell
smoothly and cleanly
through the hoop.
Gus had made a basket!
It was his first day
of practice
and his first time
on a team,
and Gus had made a basket!

"Good job, Gus!"
Pete said.
Pete was the coach.

Gus liked having a coach.
He liked being
on the yellow team.
He liked having
a bright yellow jersey
with a number on it.
He liked knowing that
when the season was over,
he would get a medal
hanging on a ribbon.
His friend Ryan Mason
told him that
everybody got one.

Gus caught his ball
and carefully dribbled it
down the court.
Then he passed it to Ryan.

Gus hoped he would shoot
lots of balls
that swished through the hoop
and made points
for the yellow team.

At Grandpa's house that weekend,
Gus played basketball
in the snow
with Grandpa's dog, Skipper.
Grandpa's hoop was old,
like everything at Grandpa's house.
The rim was bent.
The net was missing.

Gus shot a basket.
He made it!
Skipper barked.

Gus shot another basket.
He missed.
Skipper barked.

Skipper didn't know anything
about basketball.
He just knew about barking.

Gus and Skipper came in
for a snack.
"I made three baskets!"
Gus shouted.

Grandpa didn't look up
from his book.
He didn't hear Gus.

Gus tapped Grandpa on the shoulder.
Grandpa smiled.
"I turned off my hearing aid.
When there is too much barking,
I turn it off
so I can hear myself think."

Grandpa showed Gus
how his hearing aid worked.
Gus was impressed.

Then Gus shot more baskets,
and Skipper barked more barks,
until it was dark
and time to go home.

The First Game

Gus was nervous
before his first game.
He couldn't eat his lunch,
even though it was pizza,
his favorite food.
What if he missed
every basket?
What if he threw the ball
into the wrong hoop
and everybody laughed?

Gus's parents were taking Gus
to the game.
Grandpa was staying
at Gus's house
to take a nap.
He didn't like big crowds.
"Besides,"
he told Gus's parents,
"I don't think Gus needs
me and Skipper
and the Queen of England
all watching his first game."

Gus wanted to hug Grandpa.
How did Grandpa know
that Gus didn't like having
a lot of people watch him?
He wished his parents
weren't coming, either.

But they had to.
Everybody's parents came
to the games.

At the gym,
Pete put Gus in the first group
of boys to play.

The yellow team lined up
and faced the red team.
Gus shook hands with the boy
who would be guarding him.

The game began.
Gus tried to do all the things
Pete had told him to do,
but it was hard.
Everything happened so fast.
He could never shoot the ball.
The red-team kid
was always in the way.

People were shouting.

"Get open, Gus!"

Gus's father yelled.

Get open?

What did that mean?

Pete had not

taught them that.

"Rebound!"
Gus's father yelled.
Rebound?
What did that mean?
Pete had never
used that word.

"Gus, get on your man!"
Gus looked for the red-team boy
who had shaken his hand.
He couldn't find him.
So he waved his hands
in the face
of another red-team kid.
But the kid made a basket,
anyway.

At last the whistle blew.
"Subs!" the referee hollered.
At least Gus knew that meant
his group would sit down
while another group played.

Gus's heart pounded.
His head hurt.
He liked basketball practice
much better than basketball games.

Gus's team lost.
"Twelve to eight,"
Gus's father said
as they were driving home.
"Not too bad!"

Gus felt bad, though.

He hadn't made a single basket.

He hadn't even taken a shot.

He had dribbled the ball twice
and passed it once.

That was all.

More Practice

Gus and Skipper practiced harder
at Grandpa's hoop.
"Get open, Skipper!"
Gus yelled.
Skipper rolled around in the snow.
"Silly dog," Gus told him.

Now Gus knew what
"Get open!" meant.
It meant you should go
where your teammates
could pass the ball to you.
He knew what
"Rebound!" meant, too.
It meant you should grab
the ball after someone
shot and missed.

But Gus still couldn't do
those things.
He could do them at practice,
but not during a game,
when everybody was shouting,
and Gus's father was shouting
loudest of all.

The yellow team
had lost every game so far.
They had lost to the red team,
the black team,
the green team,
the purple team,
and the gray team.
Gus still hadn't taken
a single shot.

Grandpa called Gus inside
for a grilled cheese sandwich
and a piece of apple pie.

"You were looking pretty good
out there,"
Grandpa said.

Suddenly Gus wanted Grandpa
to come to the last game.
He was sure Grandpa
wouldn't shout
"Get open!" or "Rebound!"
or "Get on your man!"
Grandpa wouldn't yell
anything at all.

"Do you want to come
to my last game?"
Gus asked Grandpa.

"Do you want me to come?"
Grandpa asked Gus.

"Sure," Gus said.

"Then I sure do," said Grandpa.

The Last Game

Skipper didn't come
to Gus's last game.
The Queen of England
didn't come, either.
But Grandpa did.

The game began.
Someone passed the ball to Gus.
"Go, Gus!"
his dad yelled.

Gus looked around in a panic
for someone to pass to.
He tried to pass to Ryan.
But a blue-team boy
got in the way.

"Rebound!"

"Get open, Gus!"

"Get open!"

Gus didn't want to get open.

He wanted to sit down and rest.

He wanted to go home.

Finally the whistle blew

for subs.

Gus sank down on the bench.

He felt a hand on his shoulder.

It was Grandpa.

Grandpa pointed to his ear

and smiled.

Gus understood.

Grandpa had turned off

his hearing aid.

Then Grandpa reached down
and pretended to turn off
something in Gus's ears, too.
Gus smiled at Grandpa.

When Gus went back to play,

he tried to turn off his ears.

He watched the ball.

He watched the blue team.

He got open.

But no one passed the ball to him.

Ryan shot and missed.

Gus grabbed for the rebound.

He got it!

The crowd was yelling even louder now.
Gus kept his ears turned off.
Should he shoot?
Would he miss?
He might as well try.
He shot.

The ball teetered on the rim.
It went in!
The yellow team had won!

Gus turned his ears back on.
The noise felt good now.
Daddy and Mommy
and Pete and Ryan
and Grandpa
were cheering
and shouting
and stamping
for him.

Gus looked at Grandpa
and grinned.